This
Treasure Cove Story
belongs to
TCS
TCS

ALICE IN WONDERLAND

A CENTUM BOOK 978-1-912396-67-2
Published in Great Britain by Centum Books Ltd.
This edition published 2018.

5 7 9 10 8 6 4

Centum Books Ltd, 20 Devon Square, Newton Abbot, Devon, TQ12 2HR, UK.

www.centumbooksltd.co.uk | books@centumbooksltd.co.uk
CENTUM BOOKS Limited Reg.No. 07641486.

A CIP catalogue record for this book is available from the British Library.

Printed in China.

centum

A Treasure Cove Story

Walt Disney's

Alice in Wonderland

Pictures by Walt Disney Studios.

Adapted by Al Dempster from the motion picture based on the story by Lewis Carroll.

Alice was growing very tired, listening to her sister read. Just as her eyes began to close, she saw a white rabbit hurry by, looking at his pocket watch and talking to himself.

Alice thought that was very curious indeed – a talking rabbit with a pocket watch! So she followed him into a rabbit hole beneath a big tree.

And down she fell, down to the centre of the world, it seemed.

When Alice landed with a thump, the White Rabbit was just disappearing through a door which was much too small for her.

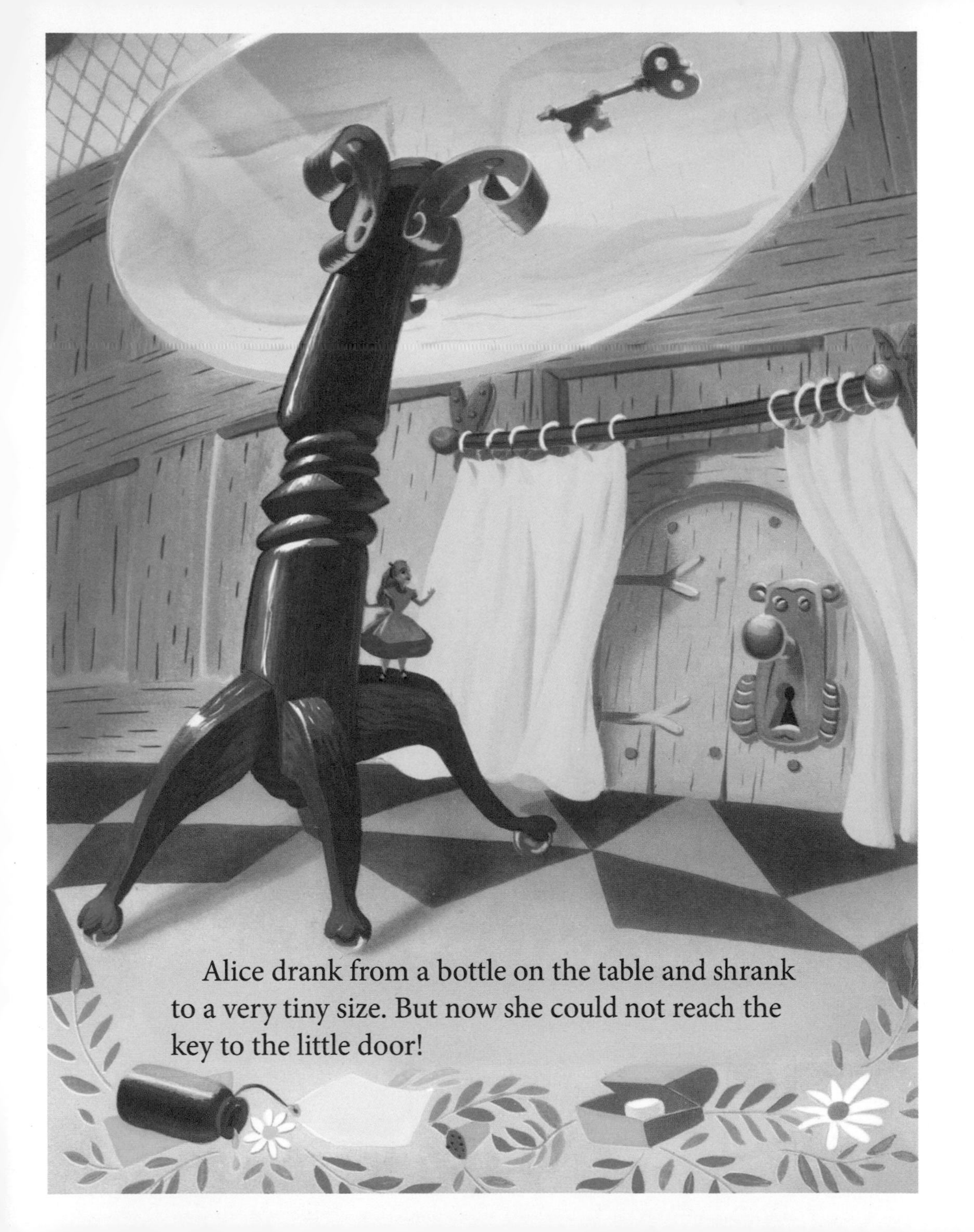

Alice drank from a bottle on the table and shrank to a very tiny size. But now she could not reach the key to the little door!

At last Alice found a way to get through the little door. Seated on a bottle, she floated into Wonderland on a mysterious sea.

On through Wonderland Alice went, looking for the White Rabbit. She met two jolly fellows, Tweedle Dum and Tweedle Dee. They did not know the White Rabbit, so Alice hurried on.

At a neat little house in the woods,
at last she met the White Rabbit himself!

The White Rabbit sent Alice into his
little house to hunt for his gloves. But instead she
found some cookies labelled Take One. So she did.

The cookie made Alice grow as big as the house. What a sight! White Rabbit and his friend Dodo thought she was a dreadful monster.

Alice picked a carrot from White Rabbit's garden. Eating it made her small again, so small that she was soon lost in a forest of grass.

Alice found herself in a garden of talking live flowers. There were bread-and-butterflies and rocking-horseflies, too.

Alice thought the garden was a pleasant place. But the flowers thought Alice was just a weed, so they would not let her stay.

Next Alice met a haughty Caterpillar blowing smoke rings. He told Alice to eat his mushroom if she wished to change her size.

Alice sampled one side, and shot up taller than the treetops, frightening the birds. But another bite made Alice just the right size.

'Now which way shall I go?' Alice wondered. The signposts she found along the path were no help – they pointed all over.

'If I were looking for the White Rabbit, I'd ask the Mad Hatter,' said a grinning Cheshire Cat up in a tree. 'He lives down there.'

Alice found the Mad Hatter and the March Hare celebrating their un-birthdays at a tea party. She joined them for a while.

After that nonsensical tea party, Alice wanted to go home. But none of the strange creatures seemed to know the way.

Alice wandered into the Queen's Garden. Soon, along came the Royal Procession. And who should be the royal trumpeter but the White Rabbit himself!

The Queen of Hearts asked Alice to play croquet. But Alice did not like the look of the game.

'Off with her head!' cried the Queen.

Away Alice ran, while the army of cards gave chase, down all the tangled paths of Wonderland and back to the riverbank.

'I'm glad to be back where things are really what they seem,' said Alice as she woke up from her strange Wonderland dream.

Treasure Cove Stories

Please contact Centum Books to receive the full list of titles in the *Treasure Cove Stories* series. books@centumbooksltd.co.uk

Classic favourites

1 Three Little Pigs
2 Snow White and the Seven Dwarfs
3 The Fox and the Hound - Hide-and-Seek
4 Dumbo
5 Cinderella
6 Cinderella's Friends
7 Alice in Wonderland
8 Mad Hatter's Tea Party from Alice in Wonderland
9 Mickey Mouse and his Spaceship
10 Peter Pan
11 Pinocchio
12 Mickey and the Beanstalk
13 Sleeping Beauty and the Good Fairies
14 The Lucky Puppy
15 Chicken Little
16 The Incredibles
17 Coco
18 Winnie the Pooh and Tigger
19 The Sword in the Stone
20 Mary Poppins
21 The Jungle Book
22 The Aristocats
23 Lady and the Tramp
24 Bambi
25 Bambi - Friends of the Forest

Recently published

50 Frozen
51 Cinderella is my Babysitter
52 Beauty and the Beast - I am the Beast
53 Blaze and the Monster Machines - Mighty Monster Machines
54 Blaze and the Monster Machines - Dino Parade!
55 Teenage Mutant Ninja Turtles - Follow the Ninja!
56 I am a Princess
57 The Big Book of Paw Patrol
58 Paw Patrol - Adventures with Grandpa!
59 Paw Patrol - Pirate Pups!
60 Trolls
61 Trolls Holiday
62 The Secret Life of Pets
63 Zootropolis
64 Ariel is my Babysitter
65 Tiana is my Babysitter
66 Belle is my Babysitter
67 Paw Patrol - Itty-Bitty Kitty Rescue
68 Moana
69 Nella the Princess Knight - My Heart is Bright!
70 Guardians of the Galaxy
71 Captain America - High-Stakes Heist!
72 Ant-Man
73 The Mighty Avengers
74 The Mighty Avengers - Lights Out!
75 The Incredible Hulk
76 Shimmer & Shine - Wish Upon a Sleepover
77 Shimmer & Shine - Backyard Ballet
78 Paw Patrol - All-Star Pups!
79 Teenage Mutant Ninja Turtles - Really Spaced Out!
80 I am Ariel
81 Madagascar
82 Jasmine is my Babysitter
83 How to Train your Dragon
84 Shrek
85 Puss in Boots
86 Kung Fu Panda
87 Beauty and the Beast - I am Belle
88 The Lion Guard - The Imaginary Okapi
89 Thor - Thunder Strike!
90 Guardians of the Galaxy - Rocket to the Rescue!
91 Nella the Princess Knight - Nella and the Dragon
92 Shimmer & Shine - Treasure Twins!
93 Olaf's Frozen Adventure
94 Black Panther
95 Trolls - Branch's Bunker Birthday
96 Trolls - Poppy's Party
97 The Ugly Duckling
98 Cars - Look Out for Mater!
99 101 Dalmatians
100 The Sorcerer's Apprentice
101 Tangled
102 Avengers - The Threat of Thanos
103 Puppy Dog Pals - Don't Rain on my Pug-Rade
104 Jurassic Park
105 The Mighty Thor
106 Doctor Strange

Latest publications

107 Captain Marvel
108 The Invincible Iron Man
109 Black Panther - Warriors of Wakanda
110 The Big Freeze
111 Ratatouille
112 Aladdin
113 Aladdin - I am the Genie
114 Seven Dwarfs Find a House
115 Toy Story
116 Toy Story 4
117 Paw Patrol - Jurassic Bark!
118 Paw Patrol - Mighty Pup Power!
119 Shimmer & Shine - Pet Talent Show!
120 SpongeBob SquarePants - Krabby Patty Caper
121 The Lion King - I am Simba
122 Winnie the Pooh - The Honey Tree
123 Frozen II
124 Baby Shark and the Colours of the Ocean
125 Baby Shark and the Police Sharks!
126 Trolls World Tour

•Book list may be subject to change.

TCS
TCS